Sleepwalker

Jillian Powell

Illustrated by
Paul Savage

FULL FLIGHT

Titles in Full Flight

Badger Publishing Limited
26 Wedgwood Way, Pin Green Industrial Estate, Stevenage,
Hertfordshire SG1 4QF
Telephone: 01438 356907. Fax: 01438 747015.
www.badger-publishing.co.uk   enquiries@badger-publishing.co.uk

Sleepwalker   ISBN 1 85880 923 1

Series Editor: Jonny Zucker.
Publisher: David Jamieson.
Editor: Paul Martin.
Cover design: Jain Birchenough.
Cover illustration: Paul Savage.

Sleepwalker

Jillian Powell
Illustrated by
Paul Savage

Contents

Badger Publishing

Chapter 1 - Nearly There

"Nearly there," mum said.

Josh said nothing. He didn't want to be there.

There were no more street lights. Just wet fields with cows in them.

Josh wanted to be back home, in the city.

"You'll be sharing a room with Tom," mum said. "It will be like having a brother."

It will be pants, Josh thought.

Josh had only met Brian's son Tom once. But he knew he was weird.

Spookily, they shared the same birthday. But that was all they had in common.

- Tom didn't have a football team.
- He didn't know the first thing about PlayStation.

What did he do? He collected fossils. How weird was that, Josh thought. Filling his bedroom with old stones.

Josh closed his eyes. He tried to imagine his old room, back home. Except it wasn't home any more.

They were going to live with Brian and Tom in the middle of nowhere. Mum had said so and that was that. He didn't have a say.

Brian was waiting at the gate for them. He kissed mum. Then he clapped Josh on the back.

"Come on in, son," he smiled.

Josh pulled away.

"You're not my dad," he said.

"Josh!" mum said.

Brian smiled at mum.

"It's OK. Tom, why don't you show Josh his bedroom?"

Tom put out his hand to take Josh's case, but Josh held onto it.

He followed Tom up the stairs.

"We've got bunks," Tom said. "Do you want the top one?"

"Whatever," Josh said.

"I should check out your case," Tom said.

Josh opened his case. His hand slid into some slimy gunk.

The top of his hair gel had come off. There was gel all over his clothes. Tom must have done something, but when?

He looked out of the window. Tom was smiling and chatting with mum and Brian.

But it was all an act. Josh knew it. Tom didn't want him here any more than he did.

Chapter 2 - A Black Shape

In the morning, Josh lay in. Mum came and woke him.

"Come on Josh, we are all going down to the beach," she said. "You won't believe how close it is."

It was close all right. You just went out of the gate and there were the cliffs.

Perhaps the house will fall into the sea and we can go home, Josh thought.

Mum and Brian went ahead. Josh walked behind. Tom kept stopping and looking at the cliffs.

He came over to Josh with something in his hand. It was an old stone.

"Take a look," Tom said. The stone had lines on it.

"It's a fossil. Millions of years old." Tom said. "You can have it if you like."

Josh looked at the stone, then he chucked it back on the sand.

"Did Tom find anything today?" Brian asked later. "He finds lots of things.

Did you show Josh the shark's tooth, Tom?"

"Don't think he's interested," Tom said quietly.

Mum, Brian and Tom were watching television. Josh decided to take his Play Station upstairs.

He climbed onto the top bunk and turned on the bedside light. There was an odd sound. Then something black shot across the room, just above his head.

It swooped back towards him, flapping in his face. He felt its leathery wings. Josh leaped down off the bunk and stood shaking. It was a bat.

The door opened and Tom appeared.

"You OK?"

Josh stood frozen.

"Oh, it's only a bat," Tom said.

"I don't care what it is, just get it out of here," Josh said.

He watched in horror. Tom went over and put his hand over the bat.

"They come down the chimney sometimes," Tom said.

I bet, Josh thought. This was another of Tom's tricks. He was so weird he probably had a pet bat.

Chapter 3 - Moon Walking

Josh was bored. There was nothing to do and no-one to hang out with. He tried to avoid Tom.

A few odd things had happened recently. Like his watch. It had gone missing on the beach one day. He knew he was wearing it in the morning. But somehow he had lost it.

"Don't worry, we'll help you find it," mum said. But Josh knew that was impossible. It could be buried in the sand. Or even in the sea.

Then Tom turned up, with something in his hand. Josh's watch.

"I found it on the beach," he said smiling.

"Oh well done, Tom!" mum said. "Say thank you, Josh."

"There you are! I told you Tom could find anything," Brian said.

He took it in the first place, Josh thought. Tom was fooling mum and Brian. But he didn't fool Josh.

That wasn't all. Josh was lying in bed one night trying to sleep. The moon sliced across his bed like a white sword. He felt the bunk beds shake. Tom was getting up.

"What's going on?"

Josh leant over the side of the bunk.
But Tom didn't answer. He just got up
and walked out of the room.
He was sleepwalking.

Chapter 4 - Strange Goings-on

The next night, it happened again. Josh was lying in bed. At around midnight, he heard Tom getting up.

"Tom?"

Tom didn't reply. He was getting dressed. Then he walked out of the room like a zombie.

This time, Josh decided to follow him.

He pulled on a sweater and some trainers.

Tom was downstairs. He reached the back door, opened it, and went out. Josh followed him.

It was dark. Tom walked along the path, then turned right at the gate. He was going towards the cliffs. Josh's heart began to race. What if Tom fell? What if this was some trick get him to the cliffs so Tom could push him over?

But Tom kept on walking. He seemed to know where he was going. He kept to the path. Josh followed him.

Then something caught Josh's eye. There was a jeep parked up on the cliff top.

Then he saw something move on the beach. There were people down there. Two of them. And a boat.

It was too dark to see clearly. Josh wondered if they were fishermen but it wasn't a fishing boat. The jeep must be theirs. He could just make out voices, but they were talking very quietly. Had Tom gone to meet them?

Suddenly Josh saw Tom coming back along the path. Tom walked past him back to the house. Josh followed, his head spinning.

Chapter 5 - Smugglers

Josh didn't tell anyone what he had seen. He waited to see if Tom would sleepwalk again. But nothing happened - until one month later.

Josh woke in the middle of the night. Tom's bed was empty. Josh swung out of bed and down the ladder. The back door was wide open.

Josh grabbed a pair of boots. Then he went up the path. Tom was ahead, walking along the cliffs. Then Josh saw the jeep, parked up on the cliff top again.

He got a bit closer.

This time, he could see better. There were three men.

One of them was taking something off the boat. The others were standing apart, talking in whispers. One man handed another man an envelope. He put it in the inside pocket of his jacket.

Then they both went down to the boat and began helping the other man.

Suddenly, there were footsteps right behind him. He swung round, his heart thumping. It was Tom.

"Tom! Did you see them? I think they're smugglers," he whispered.

But Tom was asleep. He just kept looking ahead as he walked back to the house.

Josh took another look. The men were coming up the cliff path towards the jeep. He had better go back.

Chapter 6 - Caught in the Act

The next day, Josh kept thinking about the smugglers. Tom said nothing. He knew nothing, Josh felt sure. But something was making him sleepwalk - as if he knew something was going on.

That night, Josh lay awake and waited. After midnight, he heard Tom get up.

Josh followed him out of the house and along the cliff path. There was the jeep. There were the men, on the beach by the boat.

Josh needed to get nearer. He needed evidence. Just by the jeep, a steep path led to the beach. Josh began to creep down it.

The men were unloading the boat.

"It's good stuff," he heard one say.

"Uncut."

So that was it! They were drug smugglers.

Josh was watching them closely when his foot slipped. A stone bounced down the cliff face.

The men looked up, searching the cliffs with their eyes. Then one of them pointed towards him and they began running towards the path.

Josh's heart was pounding. He had to get out of here. He ran up the path and back towards the house.

But the men were getting closer. He looked back and there was Tom, slowly walking along the path.

There was a roar as the jeep engine started up.

The jeep was going for Tom.

Chapter 7 - A Close Call

But Tom just kept walking slowly. Josh had to wake him.

The jeep was catching him up. Stones flew from its wheels as it swung towards him. Its headlights were blinding.

They were going to kill him.

"Tom! Look out!"

Josh began to run towards Tom but the jeep roared closer. Then suddenly it swung round in front of Tom.

Josh watched in horror as Tom vanished over the cliff.

The jeep braked less than a metre from the edge. Two men got out, and looked down over the cliff.

Then they got back into the jeep and drove away fast.

Josh was shaking. He raced towards the cliff edge and looked down.

A dark shape caught his eye. But it was just a rock. The beach was empty.

Then suddenly he heard a bleeping sound. There it was again. It sounded like a watch.

"Tom, Tom! Are you there? Are you okay?"

Josh lay down on the ground. He hooked his feet around a clump of grass. Then he pushed forwards so he was leaning right over the edge.

There was a ledge hidden under the cliff edge. And there was Tom, just holding on. He looked scared.

"OK Tom," Josh said. "It's me, Josh. Just hang on and we'll get you out of there."

Josh reached down with both hands. "Grab on to me," he told Tom. "I won't let you go."

And he pulled Tom to safety.

Chapter 8 -
Operation Sleepwalker

"Breakfast! Josh, Tom!"
Josh's mum stood on the stairs. She couldn't believe her ears. Josh and Tom were chatting away like best mates.

"Do you hear this Brian?

"Must have found something in common then," Brian smiled.

"Can't stop for breakfast, mum." Josh said as he and Tom appeared, then disappeared again through the front door.

They were on their way to the coast guard. They knew this was serious stuff.

- Josh had remembered the jeep number plate.
- He knew there were three men.
- He knew the dates the boat had come in.

"That's good," the coast guard said. "That gives us time to plan."

So began Operation Sleepwalker.

Josh and Tom were at the heart of it. They were there when the police closed in on the drugs ring. They had uncovered a major drugs operation.

"If I start sleepwalking again, can you stop me?" Tom asked.

"No way," Josh grinned. After all, you never knew where it would lead next!